The Girl Who Cried Rape.

Desiree Zizzo

A special thanks to my cat who helped edit this.

(Every cat owner would understand a cat's love for keyboards.)

I've always wondered why girls tried harder. They always tried harder for the guys, I guess. But the girl I wanted; she was different. She didn't try. She was naturally herself. She was naturally beautiful. I wanted her since I was in the 4th grade. Now I'm in 12th. She *never* noticed me though, even though she only lived two houses down. Every day in the morning I seen her get picked up by her friends in this little red car that sounded like it needed a new muffler. Every time I heard that loud car coming from down the street, I would run to my window just to see her for a split-second walking into the 4-door car. My mom seen me once. She made a little side joke and said, "Oh come on, just go talk to her, it's not like she doesn't know you exist." But that's the thing mom, she doesn't. My mom didn't know that though, and I wanted it to stay that way. I didn't want her to know that her son didn't have any game.

Everyday I'd walk past Brittney in the hallway. She never once looked at me. Not even a glance. I didn't know what I had to do to make her notice me. But I'd do whatever it takes to have her notice me.

One morning I didn't hear that little red car coming from up the street. So, I glanced out the window and this time I seen an all-black Camaro. I was confused so I watched a little longer, this time I seen a guy get out. Not a girl. A guy. I knew exactly who he was. His name was Derrick. Derrick Johnson. He was the biggest player of the whole school. He was the biggest jock and the biggest prick. I knew Brittney was going to get played by him, and I didn't want her to get hurt. But at the same time, I thought, maybe if she got hurt by a guy like him, she would then like guys like me. So, I thought this could be my chance. This could be where she finally notices me.

On a Friday after I got out of school me and my friend Eric went to the mall together. I wanted to go to the mall to change my style, because obviously Brittney was into 'bad guys.' While we were at the mall, I seen Brittney. Working. I decided I was going to go order a smoothie from her and see if she noticed me at all. I walked up to the counter and looked up at the menu.

"Hi, can I help you?"

I tried to hide my anxiety.

"H-hi, can I have a small blueberry blast."

"Sure, that'll be $4.25."

She still made no eye contact.

I handed her a $10 bill.

"Okay, 5 dollars and 75 cents is your change."

She began to hand me back the change. I moved my hand towards the money pushing it away.

"Keep it for yourself, as a tip."

"Really?"

Now she made eye contact.

"Yea, you look like you work hard."

"Thank you."

I saw her blush as she turned and walked away.

I turned around slickly, pointing my thumb at the situation and whispered to my friend, "Did you see that? She totally noticed me."

I could feel my face turning red and I had a huge grin on my face that wouldn't go away.

"Here you go, here's your large blueberry blast."

"Oh, I actually ordered a small."

She turned to both of her sides and looked slickly but cautious.

She whispered, "I know but this is my gift back for that generous tip." She smiled and winked.

"Oh, cool thanks!"

I walked away taking my smoothie and my friend Eric with me.

"Dude, did you see that? She totally was flirting with me!"

"I guess."

"What do you mean you guess? It was totally obvious."

"Well, I mean she was just being nice because you gave her a big tip."

"Uhm, she also smiled at me and winked; in case you didn't notice?"

"I mean, yea, I guess."

"Whatever Eric, I know what happened. I felt the connection."

I glanced over and seen Eric roll his eyes.

"You really don't believe me huh?"

"I'm not saying that, but I mean this was like the only verbal conversation or interaction you've ever had with her. So, I don't think you could feel a connection that quick, but I mean okay."

"Whatever."

I brushed his comments off because after all Eric never even liked a girl before, or even had a girlfriend, so he didn't even know what love looked or felt like.

After I got home, I tried on the new clothes I got. I honestly think I could pull this look off. Maybe she'd notice me now? I was hoping this would work. Possibly.

After weeks went by of me dressing like a 'bad guy', she still didn't notice me. Only one girl did. Her name was Jessica. And she was just eh. To tell you the truth, she creeped me out. She would chew her gum obnoxiously. Then pull some of it out of her mouth, twirling it around her finger while staring at me. She was *nothing* compared to my sweet darling Brittney.

If my new change of style wasn't working, I didn't know how I was going to get Brittney to notice me.

It was 5 months since I first seen that Camaro pull into her driveway for the first time. They've been together ever since. At first, I thought I'd give them maybe a week and he'd be done and gone. But no, it didn't work out for me like that of course. She looked so happy with him. She looked so much better, she looked better *with* him. He made her glow more, even though I thought she couldn't possibly glow anymore. I hated to admit it, but I thought he was actually good for her. I thought maybe he changed her, and maybe she changed him too.

One afternoon I was sitting by myself in the lunchroom eating a peanut butter and jelly sandwich. Well actually it was jam, grape jam, but that's beside the point. I *overheard* Brittney saying she was going to have a party at her house on Saturday because her parents were going out of town. In her words It was supposed to be "The biggest *fucking* banger that this school has had." I thought it sounded like fun, but let's face it, that's definitely not my cup of tea.

When Saturday came, it was around 9:00pm and I didn't see anyone at Brittney's house, so I figured it either got canceled or moved elsewhere so I went off to bed. I woke up some hours later to my alarm going off. I turned and reached over for my phone, to turn off the alarm. But it wasn't my phone making that noise. I then realized it was pitch black outside and my alarm never went off. It was music. I saw flashing lights coming from the little crack of my curtains and through the windows. I glanced outside my window and looked over at Brittney's house, and sure enough it was Brittney's party. I checked the time and it was 1:32 in the morning! I thought the party looked pretty fun actually, so I thought maybe I should go over there just to check it out for a minute, it's not like anyone was going to notice me anyway.

I threw on some jeans and shoes and walked over to her house. I headed up her steps and opened her blue wooden door. Instantly, a girl seen me without a drink in my hand. She grabbed me by my wrist and dragged me to the where the alcohol stood.

"Okay so what would you like? We have Vodka, Wine coolers, Margaritas, Spiked punch, Fireball, or whatever your heart desires."

"No, I'm fine, thank you though." I replied.

"Here you know what, I'm just going to pour you some punch, you can't go wrong with punch."

She threw the spiked punch into my hands, leaving some of it staining my white pajama shirt. She walked away, while I stood there by myself. After placing the punch down on the table, I thought I'd go wander around the house for a little bit since after all, I only lived next to Brittney for 8 years and I've never stepped foot on her property. I started to wander up the stairs to see if I could find her bedroom. As I was making my way up the stairs, I seen Derrick with some chick that had long brown hair. I knew definitely that that was not *my* Brittney. They walked into the third bedroom of the upstairs. I figured it was none of my business and for all I knew it could've been his cousin and he was letting her lie down somewhere. I decided to go check out the other bedrooms to see if I could find Brittney's room. When I made my way to the second, I realized that probably wasn't Brittney's bedroom either, so I concluded the last one had to be hers and Derrick was in there. As I exited the last room, I seen Britney go into the third bedroom, she stopped in the doorway as soon as she opened it.

"Are you fucking kidding me Derrick? I've been with you for 5 months! And in my own bedroom too?"

Brittney began to run down the stairs and out the front door, and as she did Derrick yelled out,

"Whatever bitch, she's better in bed than you!"

The whole party heard it. Including Brittney. I chased Brittney out the front door and explained to her that I witnessed what just happened and I asked her if she was okay.

She turned to me and said, "Thank you Dillian, you've always been so nice to me and I never appreciated you enough."

"Y-you know my name. You know who I am?"

"Yea, you've only lived next to me practically my whole life."

"Oh."

There was silence for a long minute, she turned to me, I turned to her and she leaned in to kiss me. That's when Derrick came rushing out the front door.

"Wow."

He began to clap his hands.

"We broke up 5 minutes ago and you already have another boyfriend?"

"Really Derrick? You got another girlfriend when we weren't even broken up yet."

"Alright nerd, what's up? You want my girl? You're going to have to fight for her."

I shook my head and began to studder.

"N-no I-I don't want no problems."

"Seriously Derrick? You're ridiculous, I'm not your girl anymore so just stop. Let's go Dillian."

She grabbed my arm and dragged me out to the sidewalk.

Derrick shouted from behind in the distance, "Yea, run you little wimp."

For some reason it seemed like we walked for miles when it was only minutes. We somehow ended up at my house and on my front porch. We both took a seat on my wooden porch swing.

"Look, I'm sorry about him. He can really be-"

I cut her off.

"It's fine, I totally understand. I mean you're beautiful, who doesn't want you? You deserve better than him. You deserve so much."

"You think I'm beautiful?"

"Of course, I always thought so."

That's when she leaned in for a kiss again. This time I knew she was drunk. She was so close I could smell the alcohol on her breath. But I couldn't back away. This was probably going to be my only chance to kiss her. And I had to. I had to. I've been waiting for this moment for years. And I wasn't going to back away now.

At first it was just a little kiss. A peck. But then we started making out and it eventually led to her touching me. I continued to let her because it was only fair to me. She pushed me against the bench and began to get on top of me. After about

20 minutes of making out and her caressing me she stood up.

"I'm sorry, I'm drunk and I'm kind of exhausted, I think I should just go back."

She seemed nervous, scared almost.

"Oh, I could walk you back."

"No, no I'm fine."

She took a step back as I stood up.

"Alright, maybe I'll stop by tomorrow and see how you're doing."

"Uhm, yea, yea sure."

I watched her as she walked away. After she got so far, I could no longer see her because of the darkness throughout the sky.

I walked into my house and began to scream.

"Finally! Finally!"

I saw my mom's bedroom light turn on and I remembered how late it was. I dashed towards the couch, put the blanket over me and pretended I was asleep.

The next day I woke up on the living room couch at about noon. I got myself together and headed towards Brittney's house. When I got there, I knocked on her front door. I knocked for about 5 minutes until she finally answered.

"W-what are you doing here? Why are you here? I don't think my boyfriend would be okay with this."

She seemed hysterically scared. Of me.

"I was just making sure you were okay from yesterday, and you're still with him? Don't you remember what he did to you yesterday?"

"Don't you remember what you did to me yesterday? You have some real nerve coming here after that."

"What are you talking about? What did I do?"

"You took advantage of me, while I was drunk, that's *sick*!"

She slammed the door so hard in my face that I almost forgot what I was doing here.

On the walk back home, I was trying to figure out what she was talking about. I mean I didn't do anything sexual with her. I didn't *rape* her. Maybe she confused me with someone else? Was she going to tell everyone I raped her?

I got back home and threw myself on the couch. All I could do was just sit there and stare.

"You okay honey?"

"Yea mom, I'm fine."

I couldn't tell her what happened. Would she think I was sick too? What would my mom think of me? Would she think I was just another guy who objectifies girls?

"You sure, I seen what happened, that looked a little heated."

"Yes mom, I'm fine!" I began to shout. Then I stood up and walked up to my room. Slamming the door behind me.

The next Monday when I got to school, I told my friend Eric about it.

"Well you didn't do anything right?" He asked concernedly.

"No, we were just like kissing and she touched me."

"Then I don't know that's weird? Did you kiss her, or did she kiss you?"

"She kissed me, that's the thing. She was the enabler. She started it all but, I knew she was drunk. And I wasn't, but like still dude, she did it all, I just let her do it."

"Yea man, I don't know, that's weird. I just hope she doesn't tell anyone or like calls you a rapist or something, because that would be really bad."

"Yea, I mean no one said anything yet today or looked at me weird, not even her best friend, so that's a good thing, right?"

"Yea."

We walked away and headed towards our next class. I walked past Brittney and this time she looked at me. But not in the way I wanted. I tried to call out her name, but she ignored me. I began to chase after her and I grabbed her by her arm.

"Brittney, can we talk?"

"Get away from me you rapist!"

Everyone in the hallway froze. Including Brittney. And even me. I removed my hand from her arm and backed away.

"Brittney, he raped you. When were you going to tell me about this, I'm your best friend!"

"Shut up, Jessica!"

"Rapist! Rapist! Rapist!" Everyone in the hallway began to chant.

"That's enough!" A teacher said from behind.

"Let's go, both of you, we can solve this in the principal's office!"

She separated both of us, standing in between us. It felt like my whole world was over. All at once. Just because of one little word.

On the way to the principal's office I just kept replaying the scene in my head, I kept thinking about the random people I didn't even know calling me a *rapist*.

I sat down in a chair in the principal's office as Brittney sat in one of the chairs at the front desk. Mr. Lemar closed the door and sat down in his seat. He folded his hands together, scooted in closer and looked me in my eyes.

"Alright, so do you want to tell me what's going on here?"

"I-I don't know. Honestly Mr. Lemar."

He looked at me like I was a kid who stole a candy bar and then lied about it right to his face.

"Come on now Dillian. You never get in trouble, so what happened? I know you know what happened."

"I don't. Really. All I know is on Saturday she threw a party. I went to it because I live next door, so why not? You know? So, I went over there and fast forward she found out Derrick her boyfriend, or ex-boyfriend, whatever, cheated on her. So, I went outside to go comfort her and then some-how we ended up on my front porch. Then she started kissing me and touching me. But I didn't touch her back or anything at all. So that's why I don't know why she's calling me a rapist!"

"Was she drunk."

"No, yes, I mean I don't know. I didn't see her drink. I wasn't at the party long."

I lied. I knew I lied. I knew she was drinking, but I had to make myself seem as innocent as possible.

"Were you drunk?"

"No."

"Dillian."

"I wasn't Mr. Lemar! You know me, you know I'm not like that."

"Okay, so how did the incident in the hallway happen?"

"Well the day after the party I went over to her house. Just to see if she was okay over the break-up. She asked me why I was there and how could I take advantage of her when I knew she was drunk. But I didn't know. So then today I went up to her to talk to her about it and she screamed in the hallway 'Don't touch me you rapist.' That's when her best friend Jessica chimed in. And then when she did everyone started yelling throughout the whole entire hallway 'Rapist'. That's when the teacher broke it up."

"You say Jessica was involved?"

"Yea, Jessica, her best friend."

"Alright well you can go back to class now, I'm going to talk with Brittney about this."

As I walked out of the principal's office Brittney gave me a dirty look. I looked in the opposite direction and pretended as if I didn't even notice her.

When I got home that day, I suspected the principal had called my mom. And he did.

"So, are you going to tell me what happened at school today?"

"What?"

"What do you mean what? You literally can't just forget what happened. Why are they calling you a rapist and who is?"

I sighed and went through this whole process again and told her what I told my principal.

"But you didn't touch her right?"

"No, she touched me, but I mean I did kiss her."

"Well kissing isn't really sexual intercourse or rape."

The word *rape* sounded so much worse coming from my mother, but at least she wasn't accusing me of something I didn't do.

"I know, that's why I don't get why she's doing this. It makes no sense to me."

"Probably for attention. But wow. She's lived next to us forever I wave to her parents all the time. And she's doing this? I wonder what they must think."

"What do you think's going to happen mom. Do you think I'll go to jail?"

"I don't know, I don't know if she's going to fess up and say she was lying or if she will get the cops involved."

I tilted my head looking down. I knew my life was over. I knew this would change my life forever.

The following day I went to school. Nobody wanted to talk to me. Not even Eric. He knew I didn't do it, but he didn't want to get hated on just like me. I didn't blame him though. Everyone was talking about me all day long. I heard everyone in my classes whispering loud enough for me to hear.

"Yea he raped Brittney, you didn't know?"

I got dirty looks from girls all day, and guys threatening to beat my *'ass'*. What did I do to deserve this god? I didn't do anything. All I did was kiss the girl and now I'm a *rapist*?

At the end of the day I went to my locker to put my books away. And just like you see in the movies the word *rapist* was spray painted onto my locker. I never thought something like that happened in real life. But it did. And it happened to me.

When I got home, I told my mom what happened. And she was furious. She started looking into other schools to send me to so that I would no longer get harassed. She also called the school and demanded to speak with the principal. The phone call lasted about 5 minutes and I mostly only heard my mom yelling and screaming. When she got off the phone, she informed me that they will be putting me in the credit recovery room for the whole day because there are very few people in there, so I won't have to interact with many people. My mom basically thought it was a stupid idea because I was innocent so why should I get punished and time taken out of my classes but, it was the only thing they said they could do. They also said that they would make an announcement tomorrow on the intercom about bullying and if they don't know the story don't tell the business. He said he was going to talk to me tomorrow so I could give him the names of people doing this. The names? I don't even know half the people that are harassing me! And if I did, then that'd be like 300 names!

I went to school the next day and it was basically a repeat of the day before. Yea, I wasn't getting harassed all day long, but on the bus ride I was, and on the way to my one classroom I was. I basically ran to my class so I wouldn't have to deal with this any longer. Why would she do this to me? Why would she lie? For attention? She had enough attention already. Was it because she was hurt from Derrick? Did Derrick put her up to this? I was actually surprised Derrick didn't say a thing to me yet or show up at my house. But as I thought about it, I didn't remember seeing him at school at all. Maybe she was planning to do the same thing to him? I just wish I knew what was going on in this girl's head.

Later that school day Mr. Lemar called me down to his office.

"Alright Dillian. So, what's going on? Who's bullying you?"

"Well, I wouldn't call it bullying."

"Are they threatening you?"

"Yes."

"Are they calling you names?"

"Yes."

"Are they getting physical with you in any way?"

"Yes."

"Okay, then that's bullying."

"I mean, yea."

"So, who's doing it, what are they doing?"

"It's too many people to name and count. But it's both guys and girls. The guys shoved me threatened to beat my ass. The girls have been repeatedly calling me a *rapist*. And yesterday when I got to my locker someone spray painted the word *'rapists'* on it."

"Yea a teacher noticed that and one of the janitors are working on repainting it now. Do you know who did that?'

"No not at all."

"Okay, well can you at least give me the names of the people you do know that have been verbally, and physically harassing you."

I began to give him my long list of names. I think I gave him about 20-30 names.

"Wow. Well uhm I'll call these kids down one by one, talk to them as well as notifying their parents."

"Alright, thanks Mr. Lemar, you're a great help."

I lied, but it would've been better if I lied because then he'd actually believe he was helping me.

On my way back to my one little classroom, the bell rang, great. Just my luck. I tried to rush and speed walk, but of course some jocks caught up to me. They shoved me into a locker and picked me up by the neck of my sweater.

"Where you going huh? To rape another girl?"

I moved my head turning away from their faces. And as I did, I seen Brittney walking past. Watching me get terrorized.

"Hello, rapist, look at me, not some random girls."

He forced my neck to turn towards his face.

He laughed sarcastically and then spit in my face. He let go of my sweater and kicked me in the balls. He walked away leaving me and his spit sliding down. I looked up and seen Brittney, frozen but still staring. Eventually one of her friend's came by and took Brittney with her.

I sat there against the locker for a while until some teacher came my way to help me up.

"Are you alright? What happened?"

She grabbed a tissue from her pocket and wiped the saliva off of my face.

"I just want to go see Mr. Lemar."

"I think you should see the nurse."

"No!" I shouted. "I want to go see Mr. Lemar."

"Alright fine, I'll take you to him."

She helped me up and walked me over to Mr. Lemar's office.

"Oh, Dillian, Dillian, Dillian."

"I can't do this anymore Mr. Lemar. I've gotten so many threats and physical abuse over like a period of 3 days!"

"Who did this to you?"

"I don't know his name, someone on the football team."

"Well, he definitely won't be on the team much longer."

I began to moan and groan of pain.

"Alright Dillian, we can talk about this tomorrow, after school hours, me you and your mom will have a meeting. For now, I'm going to call your mom to come pick you up."

"My mom's not here. She left this morning out of town for work. She'll be back sometime tomorrow though."

"Alright, then I guess I will call your mom and explain to her what happened and ask permission for you to go home."

"Well, how well I get home?"

"I'll take you. I'll ask her if I can take you."

"Okay."

While he was on the phone with my mom, I could hear my mom screaming through the phone when he told her what happened. After the phone call was over, he told me that she said it was fine to take me home. He also told me that she was very mad about the situation and she wanted something done about it. He continued to tell me on the car ride home how he's sorry he hasn't taken more action and responsibility but he's going to try everything in his power to fix this. A part of me wanted to believe him, but I knew nothing was going to get done about this.

When I got home, I decided to take a nap because the pain was still too much to bear. Before I took a nap, I scrubbed my face with dawn dish soap as hard as I could. Even after I could still smell the stench of his saliva stuck on my nose.

I eventually fell asleep and woke up to a knock on my door. My mom was home already? Why would she be knocking? I walked over to my front door and I opened it. I really hoped I was still sleeping, and this was just a dream. Why was she here? To accuse me again.

"What are you doing here Brittney? I don't think you should be here, it's not a good idea."

"I know, I know. I'm just here to say I'm sorry. After you left today, I went down to the principal's office and told him I was lying. He then made an announcement to everyone and told everyone to stop bullying you and that you were innocent. I told them that I didn't mean what I said, and that it came out wrong. So now no one think's you're the bad guy anymore. I just, I couldn't stand to see you get beat up like that. When you did nothing. You didn't deserve that at all. And I-I just came here to apologize. To tell you I'm sorry and that I confessed."

She then pushed through me and welcomed herself into my own home.

"Okay, but I think you should go."

She looked at me, turned her head towards the couch and sat down.

"Brittney, seriously. I think you need to go."

She then began to hide her face into the palm of her two hands and began to cry.

"Come on Brittney really?"

The only response I heard was her whimpering.

I took a seat next to her on the couch and began to comfort her. I put my hand on her back and started to rub my hand around.

"I'm sorry Dillian, I really am."

It felt genuine. Like she was actually sorry. Like she meant it.

"It's alright."

She turned to me and buried her face into my right shoulder. She cried for minutes which felt like hours. I let her and didn't say a thing. After a while I noticed she stopped crying, but her head remained lost in my shoulder.

Brittney lifted her head just a little and began to kiss on my neck. She pushed me down leaving me lying on my couch. She unbuckled my belt and pulled down my pants. I knew this wasn't good. But I couldn't stop it. I didn't want to stop it. I mean, she wasn't drunk this time so she couldn't say I took advantage of her and she's the one making all the moves again. And as a bonus her apology was genuine.

Brittney continued to undress me and herself. And I continued to let her. After 10 minutes of this she pulled a condom out off the pocket of her sweater.

"Here put this on."

She threw the condom onto my chest.

"W-what?"

"Put it on!" She yelled.

"Alright."

I put the condom on and after 20 minutes of us doing after marital things, she got up and sat at the end of the couch.

"Are you alright?" I asked.

"Yea, I'm fine."

"You sure? You don't seem fine."

"I said I was fine!"

"Okay."

I picked up my underwear, pants and belt and started to redress myself. She starred as I did this.

"You were right, this wasn't a good idea. I should go."

She grabbed her clothes, threw them on, leaving her T-shirt inside out. I watched her as she ran out my front door slamming it behind her.

What did I do? Was I not good enough? Was I too good? Did I say something? Did I not say something?

I didn't know what happened or why it happened. It just happened. I started to wonder if she was crazy or if it was just girls.

Later that day I seen her parents leave their house. I walked over to Brittney's and knocked on her front door.

She didn't answer so I started to walk back to my house. On my walk back I turned around and glanced at her house one more time. That's when I noticed the curtain move in her living room. I knew that was Brittney and I now knew she was avoiding me. On purpose. Was this going to happen all over again? Was she going to lie again?

I was so scared for the next day of school.

I couldn't sleep all night long. I was tossing and turning, letting my anxiety take over. I didn't know what to expect tomorrow at school.

The next day at school the first thing I did was talk to Mr. Lemar. I told him what happened yesterday, and he told me that wasn't a good idea because of what she had just accused me of. I agreed but confessed I didn't want to stop it.

After I left his office, I started to walk back to my one classroom of the day. As I was making my way there, people still continued to call me a rapist. Brittney was right there. Watching. Listening. And she did nothing to stop it. As I walked past her, I turned around and watched her go into the principal's office. I thought to myself that she was probably going to tell Mr. Lemar what she just saw and help me out. But that's not what she did. Not at all.

Later that day I got called down to Mr. Lemar's office. When I walked into his office, he definitely didn't seem too excited to see me. He actually looked disappointed. In me.

"Yea Mr. Lemar?"

"I told you it wasn't a good idea, didn't I?"

"What? With Brittney."

"Yea, you might uh, you might want to take a seat."

"Alright."

I took a seat and looked up at him as he starred out the window.

"So, what happed Mr. Lemar?"

"Well, she's saying you actually raped her this time."

"What!" I yelled out of anger.

"Yea and she also threatened to go to the police if I don't kick you out."

"So what? I either get kicked out of here or go to jail?"

"Pretty much, but we don't have any solid proof or any reason to kick you out so we can't do that, but if we don't, she'll go to the police."

"So now what?"

"I'm going to have to call your mom and her parents and have a meeting with all of you together."

"Th-that's not a good idea, her dad will kill me."

"Well that's the only solution I have. Maybe if we all sit down and talk maybe she'll confess. Look Dillian, I know you didn't do anything wrong. You're a good kid. However, Brittney, she's always been little Ms. Popular. And she's always cried for attention. But I never knew she'd take it this far."

"Yea, me neither."

After our conversation ended, he dismissed me back to class. I was so tired of Brittney doing this. Was she mentally ill? Was she just alone and wanted attention? I mean, who does stuff like this?

15 minutes before school got out, I was called out early by my mom. I walked to the main entrance and we headed out of the building.

"*Rapist.*" One of the front desk ladies uttered.

"What did you just say?" My mom took a step back and looked over at her.

"N-nothing." The lady stuttered.

"You better have not said nothing to my son, I mean that's ridiculous grow the *fuck* up."

My mom dashed back into the main doors and through the hallways into the principal's office.

"Mr. Lemar! Mr. Lemar!" She shouted.

"Hi, Ms. Smith, uh what are you doing back?"

"Well let's see, the lady up front, yea well as we were walking out of the building, she had the nerve to call my son a rapist! I'm so tired of this school and nothing getting solved! She's supposed to be a role model for these kids but yet she's saying stuff like that. This isn't okay, and if you don't do something about it, I will call the board and file a complaint!"

"There's two ladies up front, could you describe her?"

"The one with glasses, and blonde hair."

"That would be Ms. Petcha."

"Yea, well whoever she is, she needs to be fired and out of here!" My mom, still shouting.

"I'll get it handled Ms. Smith. You won't see her again after today."

"Let's go Dillian, this is obviously not a safe environment for kids."

I followed my mom as she stormed out of the principal's office. When we made our way back to the main entrance, my mom was still obviously mad.

"I should spit on you for talking to my son that way."

I continued to follow my mom as we walked out the doors. I watched as Ms. Petcha starred in fear.

"I mean this is ridiculous, that was just unacceptable."

I listened to her rant the whole way home. Yea I was upset too, but I sort of learned to ignore it.

After we got home my mom was still going on about what happened.

"Mom, that's enough! I listen to drama all day at school, I want to come home to a positive environment where I don't have to hear stuff like this anymore!"

"You're right. You're totally right, I'm sorry."

After a long minute of awkward silence, I ran up to my room. As I ran up the stairs I screamed out,

"Please don't bother me, I want to be left alone."

I eventually fell asleep and woke up from my mom banging on my bedroom door.

"Hey, Dillian, we have to go to the school to have a meeting with Mr. Lemar and Brittney and her family. You need to get up."

A couple minutes later she came knocking again.

"Dillian, come on you need to get up and ready. Let's go!" She yelled.

"Okay!" I yelled back at her.

I somehow managed to get myself up and out of bed. I wanted to wear something nice, but not too nice but also not too immature. I wanted to look innocent. Like a good person. I hope her family knew I was innocent, but of course they'd believe their own daughter over some guy.

I threw on a nice, black button up shirt and some jeans. I headed downstairs and there my mom was, waiting for me. We jumped in the car and headed to the school. When we got there Brittney and her family were already in Mr. Lemar's office.

"Good morning, Ms. Smith and Dillian." Mr. Lemar said with a slight smile on his face.

"Good morning." My mom said back quietly.

I looked up at Brittney and her family and noticed they were all giving me dirty looks.

"Dammit boy, what'd you do to my little girl?"

"Mr. Hills please, were here to talk and hear both sides of their stories."

"Alright, fine."

"Okay, you can all take a seat now."

He pointed in the direction of our seats.

We all took a seat and starred at Mr. Lemar waiting for him to start the awkward conversation that was awaiting to happen.

"Alright so as you all know, Brittney claim's Dillian raped her."

"Not claims, he did." Brittney lied, confidently.

"I'm talking Brittney. So, in case you didn't know Mr. and Mrs. Hill's, last week when you left out of town, Brittney threw a party. And this is when she first accused Dillian of rape. This incident you did not know about because she begged and begged me not to tell you and that she'll tell you guys when she was ready. Then about two days later she said she made it all up. Then after she confessed of her 'lie', she came to school the next day saying Dillian raped her 'for real this time.' Now I don't know what to believe because she lied about it the first time, and before Brittney came and told me 'he really did this time', Dillian came to my office and told me his side of the story and that Brittney came over to his house apologizing and that she lead herself on to him."

"That's a lie! My little girl would never do something like that!" He shouted so loud I think the people in the hallway heard him.

"Which part?" Mr. Lemar asked, seriously but sarcastically.

"All of it!"

"Well I have several sources saying that she did throw a party so that part is true. Now for the other parts it's just her word against his, and since she confessed before and said she lied, it looks more worse on her part."

"I never told you I lied!" Brittney, once again, lying.

"Brittney, come on now, why would I be lying, I'm here to solve this problem before it gets out of hand."

After hours of us arguing and telling our side of the stories, Brittney still kept her claim.

"Alright, well I know my little Brittney wouldn't lie about something like this. Anyway, Dillians always been a creep, watching her through his window every time she'd go outside."

He saw me?

"So, I think we're going to the police about this, thanks for solving nothing and wasting my time. This kid could have been arrested already. Let's go!"

He walked out the door leading his lying daughter and silent wife with him.

"So now what? Dillian's innocent and now he's going to go to jail for something he didn't do?"

"One, Ms. Smith, thank you for being patient and calm."

She shook her head in an understandable way.

"Two, I will give the cops my side of the story and tell them how she confessed she lied before. This will look worse on her part than his. The only thing is, girls usually win cases like these, because well, they're girls,"

"Yea, and it's sad because he's innocent and there's nothing we can do. But thank you Mr. Lemar. I'm sorry for all this."

"Not your fault. I'm sorry, I wanted to hold this meeting so that they wouldn't go to the police. But they're still going."

"You tried. And you're the only one who believes my son. I couldn't ask for more."

My mom shook his hand and looked at me in urge to do the same.

"Thanks Mr. Lemar." Then I shook his hand, griply.

We walked out of the building and I missed school, once again.

When we got home my mom started to talk to me about what may happen.

"If they do arrest you on her charges then when they question you, do not tell them anything. I promise I will get you a lawyer son. You won't go to jail for something you didn't do. I promise."

I listened to her continuing to promise what she couldn't control, and I acted as if everything was fine. But I didn't want to tell her the truth, I didn't want to tell her I was going to *jail*, and her only son was going to get taken away. My mom didn't want to know it, but I knew it.

I sat on the couch with my mom for a while watching movies. She got lost in the movie, but I was still nervously waiting for the cops to knock on my door and take me away.

My mom eventually fell asleep on the couch around 5:00pm leaving me awake all alone. About 30 minutes later I heard a car a house down and seen two headlights. I looked out my window and Brittney and her parents had just pulled in their driveway. I got more anxious than I ever have this whole week. I knew they just got back from the police station and they would soon be here to arrest me.

I sat against the couch next to my mom waiting for that knock on the door. I eventually fell asleep and woke up to my mom screaming and pleading,

"No, don't take my son away, please. He's innocent, you can't."

As soon as I got up and turned around, I seen the police standing in my doorway. Pushing my mom away asking where I was.

"I'm right here." I yelled.

"Dillian no!" My mom cried and pleaded.

"Mom, I'm innocent, I'll win this, I'll be back. I promise."

I promised something I couldn't control. Just like she did. And she knew my promise was something I couldn't keep either.

As I got driven away in the back seat of a cop car, I seen my mom on her knees. Pleading to god, crying. Her only son was gone. The only one she had was gone.

I felt like I betrayed my mom. All I could think about is how could I do this to her? I left her all alone and she had nobody. Nobody at all. She didn't talk to her parents because they thought she had me way too young with some jag off. And he was. My 'dad' was a jag off because he left her. But now I left my mom too. Was I just like my father? Would my mom forgive me?

Two minutes after I got thrown into a cell my mom came running into the station.

"Where is my son? Where is he!"

"Ma'am you have to wait, we have to take him into questioning. If he doesn't confess, we have no solid proof he did this, so therefor he will be able to go home tonight but we will have to schedule a court date involving both Brittney and him."

"No, no he's not answering any questions!"

"Well, if he refuses to answer any questions, that makes him look guilty. We just want to hear his side of the story."

"Can I talk to him? Before he goes into questioning."

"Fine. But only for 3 minutes."

I watched as the officer lead my mom to me.

The officer stayed in the room and watched.

"Do you have to be here?"

"Yes ma'am, I wasn't even supposed to let you do this, but I did. I have to make sure you don't hand or take anything from him or tell him information that shouldn't be said."

"Alright then."

My mom looked slowly away from him and then at me.

"Dillian, I talked with the officer. Just tell him your side of the story. Tell him what really happened. It'll be better on your part because you're cooperating."

"Okay mom." I saw the anxiousness and worry that filled my mom's eyes.

"Mom don't worry. I'll be fine. I should be home tonight."

"I'm not worried, I know you'll be home tonight."

I knew she lied. I knew she was worried. I was too. But I had to make her think I was confident and knew what I was doing.

"Alright. Your three minutes are up. Let's go."

"I love you son. I'll be here all night long. Waiting."

She grabbed my hand tight and looked me in my eye.

"Hey, no touching!"

He ran over grabbed my mom and I's hand and made sure we had nothing.

"Alright let's go!"

I watched my mom walk away slowly and painfully.

I sat in the cell a long while until one of the detectives came to question me.

"Alright Dillian, I'm going to take you into questioning. I got permission from your mother."

He walked into the cell, put me in handcuffs and walked me over to the interrogation room.

"Alright, take a seat son."

I took a seat, folded my hands and looked up at the detective.

"So uh, I'm pretty sure you know why you're here."

"Yep." I sighed with irritation.

"So, Brittney claims you raped her, two days ago. Is that true?"

He moved his glasses a little down his nose and looked up at me.

"No sir."

"Did you see her at all that day, which was September 16th."

"I saw her yea. She came over to my house. My mom wasn't home. Before she accused me of rape *this* time, she accused me of sexual assault, and rape a couple days before. She then told my principal she made it up and then she showed up at my house, this was still on September 16th. She started apologizing and one thing led to another we ended up on my couch. She took my pants off and threw a condom at me and told me to put it on. So, I did and then we you know. But I never once raped her, she never once said no, and I wasn't even the one to initiate it, she was. I knew it wasn't a good idea, but her apology seemed real, but obviously it wasn't."

"Alright, well I'll have to speak with your principal about that accusation and see what he says. But for now, how did she accuse you the first time? What happened?"

"Well, one day her parents went out of town, so she threw a party. At the party her ex-boyfriend, Derrick, cheated on her and I witnessed the whole thing. So, I followed her outside to see if she was okay and she leaned in to kiss me, but then Derrick came out and got mad. So, we somehow made it to my house, I only live two houses down. Anyway, at my house she kissed me, and we started making out and she touched me, but I never touched her."

"Hmm, okay."

He continued writing all of this down on a little white notepad.

"So, who else has heard your side of the story? Anyone?"

"Yea, principal Lemar. Mr. Lemar."

"Alright, well I'll have to contact your principal, have him come into questioning and ask him. Hopefully your story checks out twice. Until then your free to go. We will have Brittney go to a hospital and take a rape kit. That will determine whether you're innocent or not. Before you leave today, we will have to take fingerprints of your fingers and your mug shot. After that, your free to leave."

I got up and got lead out the door by the detective. They took me into the mugshot room. There I stood with a sign that showed my name, the police department I was in and some random numbers along with the date.

After we finished that up, I got my fingerprints taken. All 10 fingers. I always thought it was just your index fingers, but I guess not.

After that, they said I was free. Before I even went to my mom, I went to the bathroom to wash off my hands. I didn't want my mom to freak when she saw the ink all over them.

I got out of the bathroom and saw my mom waiting for me.

"Where were you?"

"Using the bathroom."

"Really? You couldn't come and see me first before you went and did all that?"

"Mom I was only in the cell for a couple of hours, I mean you couldn't have missed me that much."

"Still I wanted to see you, make sure you were alright."

"I am alright mom."

"Okay, I'm just making sure."

On the way home my mom and I stopped at my favorite restaurant. The only time we ever stopped there was usually when my mom felt bad for something.

"Why'd we stop here?"

"Because it's your favorite."

"Well yea, but why."

"I don't know, you deserve it. After all you've been through lately."

"Oh." I slanted a smile and got out the car.

When we got into the restaurant, I was glad nobody here knew me. I could actually feel normal for once being around a lot of people.

While I was eating, I started watching the TV that was on right in front of me. After the little football game was over, the news came on. At first, they were talking about polar bears and other stuff no one really ever payed attention to. Sadly. But after that they started saying that there is an active case going on in the town about a rapist whose name they cannot reveal because they are underage. My heart dropped into my stomach and I panicked and showed my mother.

She threw down her fork and yelled, "Let's go!"

She then screamed for a waiter and demanded the check.

When we got back into the car you could easily tell my mom was bothered. I was too but I tried not to let it get to me.

"I mean come on. Everywhere we go. How is that already on the news?"

I stayed silent the whole ride home. I was too lost in my mind to say anything at all.

When I got home, I told my mom everything the detective told me. I told her Brittney was going to get tested and I told her me and Brittney had sex, but I used a condom. My mom said since I used a condom my DNA wouldn't pop up in her DNA, so I had nothing to worry about.

I took a while off school and my mom took a while of work to be with me. She didn't want me to stay home alone and do something 'stupid'. I knew she was referring to suicide. But I wasn't suicidal. Yea I was depressed and scared and everything else, but I wasn't suicidal.

After about 3 weeks we got a call from the police department. They told my mom that we needed to come down to the station.

When we got to the station the sheriff was there waiting for us.

"Hi Ms. Smith, and Dillian."

He acted like he was disgusted. Like he didn't even want to greet me.

"So, you know why you're here. The accusation Brittney made against you. Well, Brittney took the test and your DNA did not show up. No one's did. So, she didn't get raped. By anyone. So that means you're innocent. We closed this case and informed her parents about the results. If she still continues to harass you or spread lies about you raping her, let us know and we will get that handled for you. As for now we just need you to sign some papers and you can be on your way."

My mom turned to me and started crying. She hugged me and said,

"Son, I told you. I knew you were innocent. She's always been a shady little girl."

I said nothing but continued to hug her back.

The sheriff interrupted and handed a pen and some papers to my mom first and then to me. My mom read through the papers, explained to me what it was saying and signed them. And I did the same. My mom took the papers and handed them back to the sheriff.

My mom shook the sheriff's hand and I was my mom's shadow following every step she took.

We eventually made it back home and as we passed Brittney's house, I seen her sitting. Alone. On her front porch.

"Don't even look her way son. She'll probably accuse you of something else."

I turned my head away and looked straight through my mom's dirty windshield.

Was it finally over? Was I finally free and innocent? I hope so. I really really hoped so.

After about a week I didn't see anything on the news about a 'kid' raping someone. I didn't hear from the police or Brittney. So, this was a good sign.

I was finally ready to go back to school. I hope they knew I was innocent too.

I told my mom I was ready to go back, and she insisted I stay home just a couple more days to let it die down. So, I did, to make my mom happy.

One day when me and my mom were home making food together, we got a knock on our door. Again? Was it an apology or more trouble this time? My mom dried off her hand with a towel and headed over towards the door. She opened it and of course it was more trouble. Was it ever going to end?

A police officer handed my mom a letter.

"Thanks?" My mom said confusedly.

The officer walked away and into his car, she shut the door and opened the letter. After reading it for about a minute she said,

"Wow, are you fucking kidding me?"

"What? What is it? What happened?"

"Brittney and her family. They're never going to stop."

"Why? What does it say?"

"Well apparently she's suing the hospital for messing up her DNA test results, she's suing the police station for letting you go free, and she's suing us for what you apparently 'did' to her."

I stood there and starred locking my lips together. I was speechless.

"So now what?" I questioned.

"Well, this court date says it's in two weeks. Do you just want to stay home from school until we get this all resolved?"

"Yea because I want it to be known I was innocent because if not I'll continue to get harassed at school."

"Alright."

As I continued talking to my mom about this, I kept feeling my phone buzz in my right pocket. I pulled out my phone to see what this was all about.

Everyone was messaging me, people from school, adults, and people I didn't even know. They were all messaging me calling me a rapist asking how I could do that to such a beautiful girl. How did this get out so quick? How did so many people know about this?

I checked my Facebook notification's and it was then when I realized how everyone found out about this. Brittney had posted it on her Facebook tagging me in her status. Everyone was commenting saying how much of a horrible person I was, and how I need to rot in jail.

I hurried up and showed my mom. She told me to take a screenshot of the post, all the threats, the messages sent to me and the comments. So, I did. She said we needed to print this out for proof when the court date arrives.

I untagged myself from the post and deleted my Facebook all together. I had to feel threatened every-where else in the world and now on my own phone in my own home?

Me and my mom decided we were going to go to the library to print out these screenshots.

When we were on our way to the library all I could think about was when my life got so bad.

When we got to the library that's when I saw Eric.

"Hey." I smiled.

"Uhhh, hi?" He made a confused look.

I walked away trying to ignore the whole situation as if it didn't happen.

"What was all that about? I thought you guys were best friends. Are you guys fighting or something?"

"Nope. He just stopped talking to me after all these accusation against me. I talked to him about it before she even accused me, and he believed me. But then when it got out and everyone started hating me, he started hating me too."

"Wow. Yea then he's not your real friend. I always liked him, but now. Now I don't think so."

"Yea, I know once this all blows over he's going to try to be my friend again."

"Well, that's your choice if you take him back or not."

I shook my head and shrugged my shoulders.

We headed over to the computers and printed out what we needed.

As we were on the computers, I kept seeing the same lady pace back and forth staring at me the whole time as she walked past. Eventually she came up to me and said,

"Hey, aren't you the kid who raped that young girl?"

"Uh no?"

I looked over at my mom as she stood up and approached the lady. She got closer and closer into her face as every second passed by, without anyone interfering.

"Are you seriously coming up to my son right now and asking him that? You know he's underage right and I can get the police involved and you'll get in so much trouble. But no, I'm going to solve this myself."

"Chill lady, I was just asking."

"Just asking? Just asking? Really? Because what if he would've said yes? Then what would you have said or done? Stop believing everything you read n Facebook *she's just a desperate girl who cried rape.* Once you hear it from the police, then you'll know it's real."

After about a minute or two of my mom's continuous yelling, the library staff came over to quiet my mom down.

"Excuse me ma'am, you need to quiet down. This is a library."

"No how are you going to have people in here like this? She's accusing my underage son and trying to disrespect him."

"How am I allowed here? How is your rapist of a son allowed in here?"

"Rapist? Wow really?"

My mom went in to swing at her, but I grabbed her hand and pushed her back.

"Let's go mom, she's not worth it."

I grabbed my papers and pushed my mom out the doors.

"I'm sorry about this, we won't come back." I shouted as we walked out.

"Mom, it's annoying I know, but you just have to ignore it. Stop making it more trouble than it needs to be."

"No, they're making it more trouble than it needs to be. Not me."

I listened to her rant once again on the car ride home. I finally had enough and shouted,

"Mom! Seriously! I heard enough! I'm done with it, I'm done! You're supposed to be helping me and your just as bad as them! I understand your irritation but it's enough! Your hearts in the right place but you just need to stop!"

She kept her eyes on the road and didn't say a word to me for the rest of the day.

Every time me and my mom went out in public someone noticed me. It of course started a whole scene and my mom didn't listen to what I told her when I ranted. She engaged herself into these arguments and only started more trouble. I did what I always did and pulled her off. After a while I was just tired of going out in public. Especially with her. She made me more embarrassed than I already was.

I didn't hear anything from any police officers, the Court house, or Brittney for a while. Until the day of my court date arrived.

The morning of my court date I got prepared and dressed in an all-black suit with black leather shoes. I slicked my hair to the side and out of my face. My mom wore a blue dress with matching flats.

Before we left the house, we grabbed all the papers we needed. We grabbed the printed-out screenshots, my birth certificate, my ID, her ID, and the letter from the court.

We jumped in my mom's car and rushed to the Court house. As we passed by Brittney's house, I noticed their cars were still sitting in the driveway.

"Why haven't they left yet? Do they not have to go to court?"

"No, they do, who cares let them be late, that will look bad on their part."

I shrugged my shoulders and agreed.

When we arrived at court we went through some metal detectors, talked to some people in the front and finally headed towards our court room. We waited until they called us into the room. When I walked into the room, I seen the sheriff who I talked to before, my principal and some person who I'm guessing was the person who took her test at the hospital.

Me, my mom, Mr. Lemar, the doctor and sheriff were on one side of the court room while the other side was for Brittney and her family.

I smiled at Mr. Lemar and he smiled back.

"How are you doing Dillian, haven't seen you in a while."

"I'm fine. And yea I haven't been in school because you kno-"

I got cut off.

"Court is now in session." One of the police officers on the side said.

The judge banged the on the gavel.

"Alright, officer Rodriguez, can I see the papers for this case please."

She took her glasses off and looked at the papers that was handed to her.

"It looks like this case got closed this morning so you're all free to leave."

She banged on her gavel one last time.

We all looked confusedly at each other.

"Huh?" I said.

"Well we were told to come today, what do you mean?" Mr. Lemar asked.

"It means whatever charges she had against all of you are dropped now. I don't know why. The only person that would know why, would be her and her family."

"Oh." We all uttered under our breaths. "Okay then."

We packed up our stuff and headed out. On our way-out Mr. Lemar stopped us.

"Hey, do you guys want to grab something to eat?"

"Sure, I guess we can get something to eat. Where?" My mom seemed like she really didn't want to, but she was being polite.

"Anywhere."

"Okay how about we all meet up at Zizzo's Italian restaurant? That's Dillian's favorite place."

"Sure."

Mr. Lemar jumped in his car and we jumped in my mom's.

"That was strange. Why do you think he wanted to get something to eat?"

"I don't know mom. Maybe he likes you."

"Pfft, yea okay."

"But what's even weirder is that they dropped the charges. What does that mean? That she's going to admit she lied once again?"

"I don't know, usually they drop charges because they had no proof, they knew they were going to lose, or they just lied. But it could be other things too, who knows. Hopefully we'll find out eventually."

We pulled into the parking lot of of Zizzo's and got out the car. We met Mr. Lemar in the parking lot and walked into the restaurant all together.

"Just three?" The host asked.

"Yep. Just three." My mom replied.

We all sat down, me and my mom on one side of the booth and Mr. Lemar on the other sitting across from us.

I looked at him and faked a smile.

"I know you guys are probably wondering why I asked you guys out to eat. It's because I just wanted to see how you're doing. I know you've been through a lot, so I wanted to do something special at least. I know it's not much but it's something. This is my treat."

"That's really nice of you Mr. Lemar bu-"

"Please, call me Benjamin."

"Benjamin, thank you, but I can pay for our part."

"It's fine, I insist."

My mom obviously knew she wasn't going to win this so all she could say was,

"Thank you."

"So why do you guys think she dropped the charges?"

"I don't know, I think she realized how much trouble she would get into when and if they found out she was lying."

"Yea, that's kind of what I was thinking too."

"Who knows if shell start something else."

"Well, were thinking about expelling her for the lies and trouble she's brought. So at least somethings happening to her in exchange."

I sat there and listened to Mr. Lemar and my mom talk about Brittney the whole time. I was tired of hearing about Brittney. She was getting exactly what she wanted, attention.

After about 20 minutes of them talking I actually heard silence for once, so I looked over at my mom. Her phone was what was distracting her. I looked back over at my plate of food and heard my mom gasp in shock.

"What? What happened mom?"

"Look Dillian, look at this."

I took her phone out of her hand and was shocked in what I just read. I was relieved, but scared. I didn't know what to expect next.

"What is it?" Mr. Lemar asked.

My mom then took her phone out of my hand and placed it into Mr. Lemar's.

"What the? Seriously? Again? I hope she's serious this time and stops these accusations."

"Well at least she admitted she lied to the whole world, instead of accusing him this time. It already has 130,000 shares! So now everyone will know my son was the innocent one and she was the liar the whole time."

I took my mom's phone back and kept rereading Brittney's Facebook post.

"Hi, as most of you may know I was the girl who got raped. Brittney. The only thing is, I lied. I didn't get raped. I don't know why I lied. I just did. Now I'm here to apologize and admit to all my lies.

I'm sorry Dillian. I really am. I'm going to get help. Today was court, but I dropped the charges, so an innocent man won't have to pay for something he didn't do. Dillian was always a sweet kid and he didn't deserve any of this."

My mom and Mr. Lemar continued to talk about what we all just read. But I wasn't listening. I was still in shock.

After about an hour and a half they finally got done with their conversation.

"You done Dilllian?" My mom asked.

"Yep." I thought to myself, I've been done 30 minutes ago.

"It doesn't even look like you touched anything." My mom laughed.

"Yea, I just lost my appetite that's all."

"Are you guys ready for the bill now?" The waiter came over and asked.

"Yep, I can take that. Can we also get a box?" Mr. Lemar took the bill out of the waiter's hand and pulled out his wallet.

He put the money in the book and placed it down on the table.

About 3 minutes later the waiter came and picked it up and handed me the box for my left-over food.

"You can keep the change, as a tip for yourself. Thank you, everything was great!"

"Thank you so much, you guys have a great day now!"

I hurried up and threw my food into my to-go box.

I followed my mom and Mr. Lemar as they went out to the parking lot.

"Thank you, Mr. Lemar. For everything." My mom shook his hand and I did the same.

Me and my mom separated ways from Mr. Lemar.

"That was nice of him. Don't you think?"

"Yea, he's a nice guy."

"I can't believe Brittney admitted though, especially all over Facebook where she knows she'll get hate."

"Yea, and she was getting hate. Did you see the comments? Everyone was saying she was fake, and attention thirsty, and a *slut*. They were saying they feel bad for me and how they always knew I was innocent. Like yea right, you guys were just messaging me saying how I was a rapist. Now I'm innocent?"

"That's how people are. Weird. They just flow with what everyone else is doing. But at least she's getting the hate now and you're not."

"Don't speak so soon mom, she might make another accusation and I'll be getting hated on again."

"I don't think so, especially since everyone knows she's a liar."

"Yea, I guess you're right."

I was still in shock about Brittney actually posting this for everyone to see. She was a confusing girl.

I decided to reactivate my Facebook to see if anyone was still sending me hate messages or to see if anyone was supporting me.

I looked at her old post she made about me being a rapist and that one only had 50,000 shares. I know that's a lot, but her new post of her admitting has more. Now it's at about 165,000 shares.

Instead of getting hate threats I was getting support from people. They were telling me how sorry they were that this was happening to me and they will fully support me with this.

People were putting on Brittney's page how much of a liar she was and how she needs to rot in hell. I felt bad for her, but she did this to me. And she did this to herself.

I decided I was going to go back to school on Monday. Start the week off new and refreshed.

When I got to school everyone was talking to me.

"I knew you didn't do it."

"I knew you were innocent."

"You're such a great guy."

"Brittney's such a loser for that."

I heard so many more things through-out the day, those was just the few things I remembered. And honestly, I wish they just didn't say anything at all.

Later that day I heard an announcement on the intercom how bullying is not okay. Really?

Now they want to talk about bullying. Where was that at weeks ago when I was getting harassed.

I didn't see Brittney that whole day of school. I wondered where she'd gone or if she just didn't come at all.

Weeks went by and Brittney still never showed up to school. Until Halloween came.

Everyone was pushing her, spitting on her, harassing her, and calling her names. I did nothing to stop it, because why should I?

Some girl even dressed up as Brittney for Halloween. She put on a giant mask of Brittney's face, wore slutty clothes and had a sign around her neck that said, "I got raped."

Brittney ran out of the school crying. I felt bad but not bad enough to help her. I mean she accused me of rape and allowed me to get harassed for weeks. I mean which is worse.

After Halloween Brittney showed up only a couple more times to school, but most days it ended with her running out of the school crying. While she was at school, she was mostly in the social workers office the whole day.

Every day when I woke up for school there was something all over Brittney's house. Once someone TP'd it, the next someone egged it. Another time someone even spray-painted 'liar' all over her dad's new car.

After a while I saw Brittney less and less. I never seen her go outside or ever at school. I knew she was depressed. A couple months ago she was the most popular girl at our school, and now she's the most hated.

A couple months later, I was scrolling down my Facebook feed when I got a notification. It was Brittney again, tagging me in something. I clicked on it and her post said,

"I'm sorry. I didn't mean for what happened to happen. I didn't want all this to be like this. I can't take it anymore. I'm tired of getting harassed and bullied everywhere I go. Everyday there's some new vandalism on my house or my dad's car. So, I'm going to solve everyone's problem. I'm going. Forever. I'm sorry Dillian Smith. I'm sorry."

As I read this, I noticed my heart drop. Was this her suicide note? Publicly? What was I supposed to do now? I was tagged.

I dialed my mom's number and waited for her to answer.

"Mom! Mom!"

"What? What happened?"

"I-I don't know. Brittney made a post on Facebook and it seemed like a suicide note. Like she was going to commit suicide."

"What do you mean? What post?"

"Go check."

"Alright, give me a minute."

I waited a minute for my mom to pick the phone back up.

"That's not good. That definitely seems like a suicide letter. You need to get over there now."

"No, what if it's a trick. What if she really isn't going to, she just wants me to go there alone and accuse me of something else?"

"Alright, I'm on my way home. I'll call the cops just stay home and wait for me, don't leave the house, even if you see the police show up."

She hung up the phone before I could even respond.

I was scared and anxious. Would this be my fault? Would I get blamed for this?

I waited outside on my front porch. About 10 minutes after me and my mom's phone call ended, the police, ambulance, and firetrucks showed up. My mom followed not too far behind. She pulled into the driveway and said,

"I thought I told you to stay inside."

"No, you said stay home not inside."

"Whatever." She rolled her eyes.

We both stayed on the front porch looking over at Brittney's house.

"I screenshotted her post, just in case she tries to say you tried to kill her or something stupid."

I shook my head and continued to watch Brittney's house.

After about 15 minutes I seen Brittney. Well I seen her getting rolled away into the ambulance on a stretcher.

Me and my mom looked at each other in concern.

"What do we do?"

"There's nothing we can do but to wait and find out what happened to her. I'm sure the cops already contacted her parents."

I shook my head and looked down at the ground. I went inside and up to my room and began to pray.

"God, listen. I know she did a bad thing, but she's not a bad person. Please give her a second chance and get her the help she needs. She can get better with the right help. I'm sorry I didn't do anything to stop this or to stop her from getting bullied. I just, I thought she deserved it. I'm sorry."

I got up of my knees and grabbed a towel and jumped in the shower. I cried in the shower because of how bad I felt. I felt guilt. I felt wrong. I felt like it should've been me.

That night I cried myself to sleep because of Brittney. Here she was taking over my life again and I didn't even notice.

Over the time Brittney was in the hospital I didn't have drama at all, and I didn't see anyone vandalizing Brittney's house either. I wondered if they knew about what happened considering her post.

I checked to see if her Facebook post was deleted but sure enough it was still up, with my name, untagged at the end of it. No one messaged me though or said anything horrible. Instead people were commenting under her post of how much of a drama queen she was and how she needed to just 'stop.'

It was days until we found out what happened to Brittney. We were devastated. Well I was devastated, my mom seemed more relieved than anything.

I still remember vividly how and when I found out. We didn't find out from her parents or from someone we know. We instead found out from the news cast.

I remember sitting on the couch eating chocolate covered pretzels with my mom watching the news. That day it didn't seem like there was much going on. Just the regular huge donations this one corporation gave out and the animal shelter clearing out all of their animals that weekend. But then the news women said,

"Up next, why this 17-year old girl committed suicide and how to raise awareness."

I remember me and my mother turning our heads towards one another and starring at each other blankly but still in concern.

We starred at each other until finally the commercials were over and the news came back on.

"Last Tuesday, 17-year old Brittney Hills committed suicide. Her parents, Peter and Stephanie Hills, are here to talk about suicide and to give their daughter, Brittney, a better reputation than what is told here today."

I saw the camera move to Brittney's parents.

They put the microphone up to Brittney's dad and he began to talk.

"Brittney was such a sweet and innocent girl. We had no idea this was in her head or else we would have prevented thi-"

He interrupted himself, pulled out a tissue and wiped off his tears.

"We knew Brittney was going through stuff because just months ago she told us she got raped by a boy, whose name I will not mention, but some of you already know. No one at her school

believed her so she said she lied. But she didn't lie. After that everyone started bullying her and harassing her. They started vandalizing our home and our cars and our property. Brittney couldn't go to school or even out in public. Please parents, keep a close eye on your children, make sure they're okay and not depressed. You don't want to know what this feels like. Losing your only daughter."

My mom shut off the TV completely and turned over at me once again.

"I-I don't know what to say or do. Do we send them flowers or a card or?"

"Mom, no. Yea I feel bad, but like that would make it worse. We can't do that."

"You're right. I just, I feel bad."

"Me too."

We sat in silence until I finally made my way up the stairs into my bedroom. I knew people were going to come after me now. Just because he said that on the news. Now everyone would know. I'm going to get harassed and bullied all over again. This wasn't anywhere near the end. This was just the beginning.

I decided I was going to delete my Facebook so no one can see who I was or what I looked like. I didn't want anyone knowing anything about me.

The weekend after Brittney's death me and my mother were driving down the street when we saw a huge line of cars, each having a sticker saying 'Funeral'. We both did the Holy Trinity and said Amen. That was just something we always did even if we didn't know the person. When we made our way past the car's we saw Brittney's parents in the first car behind the hearse. We realized it was Brittney in there. My mom suggested that we should turn around and follow them from a distance and wait in the car and watch Brittney get buried down into the grave. I agreed just for my own good. I thought maybe this won't make me feel as guilty anymore.

My mom whipped the car around and waited in an empty lot near the cemetery. We waited a little over 5 minutes for all the cars to enter the cemetery. After they all entered, we followed slowly behind them and waited for them all to make a complete stop. We drove a little further down the little road and watched from a distance. Nobody noticed us the whole time, but I know Brittney did. I know she saw us. I knew she knew we cared. My guilt suddenly disappeared all-together.

It was weeks until I finally got my first threat mail. Whoever it was, they knew where I lived. Which wasn't good. But why would they just send a letter? And how'd they know where I lived? Was it Brittney's parents?

I showed my mom the letter and we took it to the police station.

They told us they could try and trace it back, but it may take a while. They said, that as soon as they found out who did it, they would call us immediately.

After that threat letter I didn't receive anymore. No one at school said a word to me. No one bullied or harassed me anywhere. I was safe.

After about a month the police officer who did this investigation for us finally called us back and told us to come down to the station.

When me and my mom finally arrived at the station, the officer called us into his little office and told us to take a seat, so we did.

"How are you guys today? Anymore threat mail?"

"Were doing good. And no, no threat mail, right Dillian?"

"Nope. No threat letters."

"Well, that's good. So, about the letter you wanted me to trace back. We found who did it and he lives in town and he goes to your school. Do you know an Eric, Eric Waters?"

"Are you sure? Are you sure it was Eric?"

"Yes, I traced it back to him. He then came in for questioning and admitted right away that it was him. Do you want to press charges?"

"Charges? Mom I can't. It's, it's Eric."

"I know sweetie?"

"So, you do know him?"

"Yes, Eric was my childhood best friend, until all this started happening, then he just stopped talking to me because everyone else hated me."

"Well kid, I'm sorry but it seems like he was never really a friend then."

I shook my head and looked down at the ground.

"So then no, you don't want to press charges?"

"No, I'm sorry. We can't. We just can't. I'm sorry for making you do all this work to do nothing about it."

"That's fine, I totally understand. If you get anymore threat's feel free to bring it down here. We'll get it all handled for you. Have a good day."

He stood up and opened the door waiting for us to exit. As we walked out the police station, I seen Eric getting into his mom's car and driving off. So, it was true. He did do it.

As we got into my mom's car and headed home all my mom could say was how she couldn't believe it and how she didn't think he'd ever do something like that. I thought the same, but he proved us both wrong.

After two weeks of that incident the bullying started all over again. At school, in public, everywhere. I didn't know why they thought I was guilty again. And I didn't know how the people in public knew about me either.

I went down to Mr. Lemars office again to tell him all that was happening.

"Mr. Lemar, I don't know how this is happening to me again. Everyone's blaming me for her suicide and saying I'm guilty for rape and her suicide. Even out in public. How do they know about this?"

"You didn't see it? Brittney's parents went on some talk show and talked about how she killed herself because a boy raped her, and no one believed her. Then some rotten kid in this school made a fake Facebook and tagged you and me in the post saying you're a rapist and I shouldn't be the principal if I can't help kids. So now I'm in trouble, about to lose my job and here you are getting harassed again. We're trying to find out right now who made this account and who wrote this."

He pulled out his phone and handed it to me.

"See read it."

"Dillian Smith is a rapist and he's the one who raped Brittney. Brittney told the whole Facebook about how he raped her and no one on here believed her. You all called her a liar and an attention seeking bitch. Now look at her. She's dead because of you guys! And for the principal,

*Mr. Lemar. **Benjamin Lemar.** You're no good either. She went to you for help and you didn't help her. You're in no position to be the principal. You guys are the ones who need the help. Not Brittney."*

"I uh, I don't know what to say. Who would even make something like this? Why?"

"Don't know, my thoughts are her best friend, because no one really cared as much as she did. Not even her parents."

"Probably."

"Well, all I can say for now is maybe take more time off school, talk to your mom about this. All I can really do right now is try and find out who made that account."

"Alright."

I pulled out my phone and told my mom what happened. After about 20 minutes she came to come pick me up.

"It's happening again?"

"Yea apparently some anonymous person made a fake Facebook account and said a whole bunch of horrible stuff about me and Mr. Lemar."

"They don't know who?"

"No, they said that they're going to look into it and try and find out who did it."

"Wow, I mean what's the matter with people?"

"I don't know, Mr. Lemar says he thinks it might be Brittney's best friend, but he doesn't know for sure yet, he's going to look more into it."

My mom shook her head as in if 'yea right, like that's going to happen.'

I needed something to clear my mind up. But I didn't know how. I didn't know what to do. I had no friends, no one to vent to. Nothing.

I decided to pull out my old PS2 from my closet and I hooked her up to my TV. I turned it on and began playing. I was playing for about 3 hours and didn't even notice I wasn't thinking about any of the real-world problems. I realized this was my getaway.

My mom told me I probably shouldn't go to school for a while and wait for this all to die down. I agreed because I didn't like school very much anyway, it was obviously full of stuck up snobs.

After a couple of days of the anonymous Facebook posters status, I really started getting harassed. I would wake up to find our front porch all messed up and all over the place, our mail would be ripped up and thrown all over our lawn. People even peed on our front doorstep. I mean who would do something like that?

After about two weeks that's when I started getting threat letters in the mail. Too many to count or even go to the police for. I started getting random texts from random people that I didn't even know saying how they're going to kill me, and I'll be going to hell for raping and killing a girl. I heard raping before, but killing? How did I do that? She did that on her own.

I honestly didn't even care anymore. I knew my life was over. I knew I could no longer walk outside my house and check the mail without my neighbors screaming at me, I knew I could no longer go to school without other students harassing me, and I could no longer go to my local grocery store anymore without an elderly lady giving me dirty looks and uttering something under her breath.

No one could help me anymore. Not me, not my mom, not the police. Not even Jesus himself. Nobody.

After everything that I've been through I started questioning my faith and god himself. Was Jesus really real? If he was then why was he letting all this happen to me? What did I do? Why can't I just *die*?

I started to go to church to find the answers I was looking for but even there I was getting judged. Nobody said anything to me, but their looks told me what they really wanted to say. Nobody would shake my hand when it was time, instead they just gave me dirty looks and shook the persons hand next to me and smiled at them. Nobody would even hold the door open for me. Nothing. I now realized even church people aren't any better than anyone else.

It was weeks since that anonymous Facebook post. And I was still getting harassed. My mom said it would probably die down after some weeks, but it didn't. It only got worse. I couldn't take it anymore.

One day I was sitting in my room playing my PS2 when I heard two kids outside my bedroom window laughing. I looked out my window and they were spray painting some word on the side of my house. I ran out my room and out my front door.

"What the hell are you guys doing? You can't just come here and spray paint things on my house!"

They both walked up to me and got in my face.

"But what you gonna do about it?"

"Yea you little rapists, what are you gonna do?"

"I'm going to call the cops, that's what I'm going to do."

They both looked at each other and gave each other a look that I could easily read. I knew I was screwed.

The next thing I knew I was on the ground getting kicked and punch. I was hurled up in a ball with my arms and hands covering my face. I couldn't protect myself. There was 2 of them and 1 of me. I didn't know how to fight. In that very moment I felt like I was going to die. But I didn't want it to stop. I wanted to die. I couldn't take this anymore.

After a couple of minutes of me getting beat, my mom pulled into the driveway honking her horn. She threw her car in park and got out. She began yelling but I was too out of it to understand what she was saying. The two boys ran off together taking their spray paint with them.

My mom rushed over to me immediately crying, helping me up.

"Oh my gosh. Baby, are you okay? You're bleeding everywhere."

"Yea mom, just please don't touch me, you'll only hurt me more."

She touched my back softly and helped me into the house.

"Alright let me get you a cold rag to wash off the blood and an ice pack."

"No mom, I got this. I'm going to jump in the shower right now. Then when I get out you can help me all you want. Okay?"

"Alright. I love you, and I'm sorry this is happening to you."

I went up to my mom and hugged her tight.

"I love you too mom. I'm sorry I brought this upon us, I should've never even messed with that girl Brittney."

"Honey, you did nothing wrong. Don't be sorry."

I hugged my mom tighter and kissed her on the cheek.

I ran up to my room, grabbed a piece of notebook paper and wrote a note down for my mother to find.

"Mom, I'm sorry for all the trouble I brought recently. You don't deserve this. If you're reading this, that probably means it's too late. I'm sorry mom. I'm sorry. But just know I'm happier now. I'm not depressed anymore. I hope you can move on. You're going to need to get out of this town for a fresh start. I have spare money in my sock drawer if you need any of that. I never stopped loving you mom, and I never will."

I left the letter on my bed with a picture of me and my mom next to it. I grabbed a razor blade out of the drawer in my nightstand and headed towards the bathroom. I blasted the water and waited for the tub to fill up. I took off my clothes and jumped in the tub. This was a horrible way to go but it was the only way I knew how, and I deserved it. After all the trouble I caused my mom. I just couldn't anymore.

I began to cut myself so deeply to where I couldn't bear the pain. It hurt worse than the beating I experienced only minutes before. I continued to cut myself deeply. Everywhere. After minutes there was so much blood gushing out of me, I began to faint.

I hoped this was the end. No more me, no more trouble, no more life. It was finally over. I was dead. I was happy. I was free.

Some-how I still managed to wake up. In a hospital bed. As soon as I opened my eyes there was my mother. Looking at me with tears in her bright green eyes. Although they weren't as bright anymore. They looked glassier and more hurt than anything. I just realized I hurt my mother more than anything ever has before. She would rather go through what we've been through this past week, every day of her life than to see me attempt suicide. I knew I fucked up. I now wanted my life to end more than ever before.

"Son, oh my gosh. Nurse! Nurse!" She yelled.

"Son are you alright? Baby, why would you scare me like that? You can't do that."

"How, how did I get here. I thought I was dead."

"No, no honey. You don't remember?"

"Remember?"

"When you were in the bathroom, I went up to your room to pick up your dirty clothes. I saw the note on your bed and read it, I called 911 and rushed to the bathroom. I broke open the bathroom door and seen you. Lying there. In your own blood. You looked at me slightly and said *'mom'* under your breath. I grabbed you out the tub and wrapped clothes tightly around your arms and legs to stop the bleeding until the ambulance arrived. You've been passed out ever since. Why would you do it son? Why?"

"You know why. I don't want to talk about it right now. Please. Just let me rest."

"Okay."

My mom starred at me sitting with her hands intertwined pushed up against her lips. She starred at me and continued to cry. She eventually got up and walked out the room. She stayed close enough to where I could still hear her sobs. I knew she didn't want me to see her like that. I knew she knew it would just make things worse. I knew I was the worst. But it was too late for me to do things differently.

While I was in the hospital my 'friend' Eric showed up. My head was tilted away from the door towards the TV. I heard two slight knocks and that's when I noticed him.

"Hey." He slanted his smile.

"Hi? What are you doing here?"

"Well, your mom told me what happened. I know you'll never forgive me. I'm sorry. I just, I didn't know what to do or how to act. Because if I was friends with you then, then I'd probably be in the same position as you right now."

"Okay. So that's all you came here to say?"

"Yea, I mean, well I'm sorry this is happening to you. I hope you get better."

"Okay."

He stood, still starring at the ground.

"Alright so you probably want me to go then?"

I shook my head slightly and put an unsure expression on my face.

He headed to the door but before he could make it out, he said,

"Well please just think about forgiving me. Think about it from my position, we've been friends forever don't let this little thing mess us up."

He stood there, staring at me waiting for a response. I said nothing. He turned around slowly and finally found his way out.

Seconds after Eric left, my mom came back from the little eatery area the hospital has.

"Why would you do that?"

"Do what?"

"Why would you tell Eric? You know were not friends anymore. Why?"

"I know but I just wanted you to know people care. People love you. Even Eric. He's lost too right now. Everyone who's here for you is lost right now."

"But he wasn't here for me mom, that's the thing."

"I know, but he wants to be Dillian, you have to give him another chance. Out of all the years you guys have been friends this is the first time he's ever done something like this."

"I don't know. He was just something else I didn't want to think about and now here I am thinking about him. It's just stressing me out more. Please don't let him come up here again. Tell him I said that."

"But Dillian-"

"Mom, please! I want to be left alone."

"Fine."

My mom left, leaving me alone in my hospital room. As I sat there, I thought about opening the window. I wanted to see outside, see the sun, feel and smell the fresh air. I wanted to know what it felt like to be alive again.

As I got to the window and looked out of it, I noticed my mom. With Eric. They were talking about something, what I didn't know. Their conversation lasted for a while. I watched the whole time without them noticing. After the conversation was over my mom hugged Eric and he hugged her back. Then Eric walked out, into his car and my mom walked back into the building.

My own mother. My own best friend. I starred in betrayal. How could my mom do that? Eric I could care less, but my mom? When I needed her the most.

As I still stared through the window, I heard her talking to a nurse right outside my room. I jumped into my bed and pretended as if I was lying there the whole time with no knowledge of what she just did. When she made her way into my room I immediately asked,

"So, what'd you do?"

"Nothing just went for a smoke break."

"You don't smell like cigarettes."

"It was just a small short one."

"Well you were out there for a while for a 'small short one.'"

"Well I did some errands on the way up."

"Like what?"

"Why does it matter Dillian?"

"It doesn't I was just curious."

"Alright then stop asking questions."

I rolled my eyes and looked towards the TV. I grabbed the remote and turned the volume up, hinting to my mom I no longer wanted to speak to her.

Hours went by with little to no conversation made with my mother. When it eventually got late my mom said she was going to head out and she'd be back tomorrow.

A couple days went by until they finally allowed me to leave the hospital. They gave my mom papers of therapy groups and mental hospitals that have 'really good reviews' and ones that 'really help people'. My mom put the papers into her purse and thanked the nurse.

When we got into her car I immediately asked,

"Are you really going to send me there?"

"The mental hospital? No. The therapy group? Maybe. They're kids your age who are going through similar stuff, and some of them even the same thing. I think it will help you. And it will also help you understand that other people are going through the same thing as you. I need you to understand that there are other answers besides sui-"

"Mom, okay. I know. But I'm not ready yet to go and talk to people. Especially people I don't know, and on top of that tell them my problems and have them look at me like the rest of the world?"

"Honey you don't have to talk you can just listen. I'll give you a week off to just stay home, rest and I'll stay here with you. After that I think I'm going to send you to the therapy group. I'm going to look into it later."

"Mom, I don't want to go!"

"Oh well! I'm the parent, you're the child. You're going whether you like it or not."

I sighed in anger and in irritation and every other negative emotion I could possibly feel. I looked out the window and crossed my arms.

Doesn't she want me to be happy? Then, why is she doing this? She should just let me stay home for the rest of my life.

A week went by of me staying home playing videogames. It went by so quickly I forgot I was depressed. After all, videogames were my escape.

I went downstairs on a Saturday night to eat dinner with my mother.

Immediately at the dinner table she said,

"You probably forgot all about it, but I signed you up for the therapy group. You meet every Tuesday and Thursday at 4:00pm. They're all kids in your age group aging from 15-18. I made sure none of the kids went to your school. So, you have nothing to worry about. You'll know nobody there."

"Mom I told you I didn't want-"

"I don't care what you want. It's what I want. And I want you to go. I know you don't think this will help you, but it will I promise. And if it doesn't after 3 weeks then I'll take you out of it immediately. Okay?"

"Whatever."

I bit into my chicken leg when I heard a knock at the door.

Me and my mom looked confusedly at each other. We walked to the front door together and I watched as my mom opened it.

"Oh, hi Mr. Lemar."

She opened the door wider for both of us to fit in the doorway.

"Hi Ms. Smith, and Dillian. How are you doing?"

"I'm fine."

"Is it okay if I talk with Dillian alone Ms. Smith?"

"Of course."

My mom walked away, and Mr. Lemar and I stood there at the doorway.

"Hey Mr. Lemar?"

"I heard about you know, and I'm sorry. But that's not the right answer. I just wanted you to know I found out who made the anonymous post. It was Brittney's best friend. She is now expelled from the school. I also made sure we enforce our school policy that we will not tolerate any bullying and if we see bullying of any kind going on, they will also get expelled immediately. I also wanted you to know that I have not heard any rumors about you lately at all or even heard your name. We made sure that every single kid at our high school is aware of these consequences. You have nothing to worry about when you come back, and I can promise you that. I don't want you to attempt what you did two weeks ago ever again."

"Thank you, Mr. Lemar. Thank you so much."

"No problem, can you get your mom for me please."

"Yes, I can."

I turned around and walked into the kitchen to find my mom hunched over, eavesdropping.

"Well since you were listening, I think you know that Mr. Lemar wants to speak with you."

"What? I wasn't eavesdropping."

"Yea okay."

She stood up straight and headed towards our front door.

I sat down at the kitchen table and began eating. They talked so long I almost finished eating the rest of the food my mom had made.

I heard the front door finally close and I heard my mom say from a distance,

"What a nice man, don't you think Dillian?"

"Yea but mom why are you telling everyone I tried committing suicide? I don't want people to know."

"Because he had to know in order to keep a better eye on you at school. Don't you see now you can go to school safely. Something actually got done. You should be happy."

"Well I guess when you say it like that then yea, I see where you're coming from. Thanks, in a way I guess."

She stayed quiet and finished her plate of food. After she was done, I helped her put the food away and I apologized to her and told her I was sorry for scaring her like that and I promised to never do it again. Ever. No matter how much pain I was in. She cried and hugged me tighter than I've ever been hugged before. I cried too. I knew I caused this pain in my mother.

About a week went by until it was my first therapy meeting.

As I walked in everybody starred at me. Sort of like 'Why is this guy here? Just so another person can hear about our horrible lives?' I knew this wasn't going to help me in any way possible. But I did this. For my mother.

"You must be Dillian?"

"Yep, I'm Dillian."

He reached out for my hand and I took my hands out of my pocket and reached for his.

"Wow. Nice hand shake you got there. Anyway, I'm the one who made and put this group together. I'm Mr. Geller. In this group we pretty much just talk about our problems, why we're here, our goals and anything you wish to talk about. And if you don't want to talk then you can just listen."

I shook my head and said nothing.

"Oh, you can take a seat. It looks like there's a seat open next to Abby."

He pointed me into the direction of the unclaimed chair.

I walked over and took my seat. As I sat, I noticed Abby looking at me and I looked back at her. She smiled and I did a slight smile back.

"Alright everyone. We have a new person here today. Dillian, why don't you introduce yourself?"

"Alright uhm, I'm 17 years old. I'm a senior in high school and yea that's really it."

"Why are you here Dillian."

"Just problems I don't really want to talk about."

"It's alright, were all close here, you'll eventually get used to us and tell us. So, what are your interests?"

"Nothing really. I play videogames. That's about it."

"Oh, really Abby plays videogames too, right Abby?"

"Yea, I do. What console do you play on Dillian?"

"PS2."

"Me too! We should play sometime!"

"Yea sure."

"See look, already making friends." Mr. Geller laughed softly.

"Yea." I responded unsurely.

"Alright everyone well-"

Mr. Geller continued to talk but I dazed out into my own mind not really caring what he had to say.

"Dillian! Dillian! Dillian!" Mr. Geller waved his hand in my face.

"Huh?"

"You can go now. The meeting is over."

"Really?"

"Yea, everyone else already left."

"Oh, wow. Sorry. Thanks!"

I began to walk out as I heard Mr. Geller shout,

"Don't forget about Thursday!"

As I almost made my way to my mom's car, I heard a girl from behind calling my name.

"Dillian!"

I turned around and it was Abby.

"Oh, hey Abby."

"Hey, I wanted to get your gamer tag so we could play together, is that cool?"

"Yea sure. It ChillDill23."

"Cool, I'll add you today."

"Alright, see you Thursday."

I jumped into the passenger seat of my mom's car.

"Ooh, a girl? She's pretty. Who was that?"

"I don't know, some girl named Abby."

"Just some girl?"

"Yes mom, just some girl."

We both stayed silent the whole way home.

As soon as I got home, I hopped on my PS2. Right when I turned it on, I saw a friend request from Abby. I accepted it and she later sent me a message.

"Hey Dill, It's Abby. Do you play modern warfare 2? Do you want to play?"

"Sure."

She invited me to a game and we both had a mic, so we both began talking to each other. We started talking about the group were in and about our towns and other stuff you talk about when you first get to know somebody. She was actually pretty cool. Really cool actually.

We played together all day and all night. It went on for weeks. We would talk at the meetings all the time and goof around. We even got kicked out of one of the meetings once because we wouldn't shut up. My mom was pretty mad, I didn't regret it though.

We eventually started hanging out a lot and going to cool gaming places.

One night when I came back from being with Abby my mom wouldn't stop questioning me.

"Where were you Dillian?"

"I was with Abby why?"

"Just wondering because you didn't tell me where you were."

"Oh."

I began to head towards my room to hop onto my PS2 to talk with Abby some more. As I started walking up the stairs, I heard my mom say,

"You're not scared?"

"Scared for what?"

"Scared she might do the same thing Brittney did?"

"Mom she's not like that all."

"I'm just making sure. Just please, think before you do son."

I shook my head, turned around and made my way to my bedroom. I turned my PS2 on and started talking with Abby some more.

"So, Abby?"

"Yea?"

"I was thinking, and I think I want to tell you the real reason I'm in the group and why and what lead to it, every single detail. I know you'll believe me and won't judge me. Right?"

"You know I won't. No matter what it is. So, what happened?"

"Well I actually want to tell you in person. Maybe tomorrow? You could come over?"

"Sure, but is it okay with your mom?"

"Yea I'm sure she'll be cool with it."

"Alright then yea, it's a date."

Date? Date? She thinks it's a date. Have we been going on dates this whole time? Does she like me? Does she like me like I like her?

"Yea sure. A date. Uhm come over like 3 o'clock?"

"Yea sounds good. I'll be there."

I turned my PS2 off and ran down the stairs and shouted for my mom.

"Mom!"

"What? What?"

"Guess what?"

"Uhm you finally passed that level you couldn't get passed?"

"No."

I thought about what she was talking about and shook my head no.

"No, not that. Guess again."

"I don't know."

"That girl, Abby. Well I invited her over tomorrow."

"I don't think that's a good idea."

"Why?"

"Because I mean we just got this whole court stuff behind us and I just, I don't want it happening again."

"Mom it's not going to happen again. She's not like that, I can't just go around not trusting girls just because one did me wrong."

"Alright fine, but we will *all* be down here at the same time."

"Well that's the thing, I wanted to be alone with her just for a minute. I think I'm ready to tell her why I'm in the group and exactly how I got to that position in my life."

"You trust her that much?"

"Yea. I mean people I don't even know, know about it. So why not? The worst she can do is stop talking to me."

"I guess so. That's up to you Dillian, I won't stop you."

"Okay?"

"Anyway, just give me a little signal tomorrow and I'll take the hint and leave you alone for a couple minutes. After that I'm coming right back in the room."

"Alright."

The next day I got up early and started cleaning the whole house. Including the bathroom. I wanted it to look great. For Abby.

After about 2 hours of cleaning, my mom woke up and came downstairs.

"Wow. She must be special. You're cleaning."

"Very funny. I clean. Sometimes."

"How often is sometimes to you?"

"Oh, you know, the average person's meaning of sometimes."

"Mhm."

"Well anyway mom, I'm going to take a quick shower and you should too. Abby is going to be here in a couple hours."

"Yea, yea."

I finished my shower and got cleaned up. I blow dried my hair and slicked it back. I sprayed about 3 pumps of cologne and flattened down my shirt. Abby was going to be here any minute now, and I had to look perfect.

"Mom!" I shouted. "Are you ready yet?"

"Almost."

I walked over to our living room and sat down on the couch. I waited for a while until my mom came into the room.

"Well, where is she?"

"I don't know. I'm going to text her now."

I pulled out my phone and texted Abby.

"Hey, you still coming?"

About two minutes after I sent my text, she replied back.

"Yea, running a little late. Traffic. I should be there soon."

I told my mom the news and we sat down at the kitchen table and I helped her with the food. About 25 minutes later I heard a knock at the door. I didn't have enough time to stop and wash my hands, so I rushed to the door.

"Hey Abby! Glad you could make it."

"Hey Dill, yea sorry I'm late."

She leaned in for a hug, but I stopped her.

"Sorry, sorry. My hands. They're full of food. I should go wash them."

"Oh yea, that's fine."

"Here you can have a seat on the couch while I go wash my hands."

I directed her towards the couch, and I headed back to the kitchen.

"Mom, she's here. Go say hi while I wash my hands."

"Alright son."

I went to the sink and my mom went in the opposite direction. I could hear them talking and laughing while I was washing my hands, but I couldn't make out what they were saying.

I creeped my way into the living room and then my mom noticed me.

"Hey Dillian, we were just talking about you."

Abby laughed.

"Funny mom."

My mom winked at me and walked away into the kitchen.

"Your hands clean now?"

"Yep."

"So, what were you so eager to tell me about?"

"Well uhm. How do I say this? Look Abby, I don't want you to think different of me. I'm still the same Dillian you knew and met before. When you find this out, don't think different of me. And besides it's not like I actually did it, they just accused me of it."

"Okay?" She looked at me concernedly.

"Alright well awhile back, this girl named Brittney she threw a party. At the party she found out her boyfriend was cheating on her, and she ran out crying and I followed her, you know to make sure she was okay. Well then, we came to my house, because she lived next door and we sat outside on my porch swing that we have. We started making out, but that was all we did. I wasn't drunk either. I didn't drink at all. The next day she accused me of rape. But I didn't do it."

As I was telling her this story, I knew my mom was listening.

"She later felt bad for lying and she admitted that she was lying. Then the same day she admitted her lie she came to my house. To apologize. I let her in, and I knew I shouldn't have. But I did. She came in and my mom wasn't home. We sat on my couch. This couch, and she basically cried on my shoulder and then threw me down to where I was lying on the couch. She threw off my pants and threw a condom at me and told me to put it on. I admit I didn't stop her, and I followed her instructions, but I didn't rape her. She wanted to do it. She told me to do it. I had no intentions. It was all her. Anyway, the next day she told everyone, even the police this time that I raped her. When I didn't. And I just thought you should know Abby. The sooner the better. But I didn't do it. I hope you believe me, and if you don't. That's okay. I understand. You can leave if you feel uncomfortable."

"I know."

"What do you mean you know?"

"I mean I know. I heard about it. It was all over the news. But I knew from the start she was lying. You could tell, it didn't add up or anything. I believe you. I can tell you're a good guy."

"Why didn't you tell me sooner you knew?"

"Because I wanted you to tell me when you were ready."

"Oh. So, but you believe me, though right?"

"Of course."

"Wow, I was scared to tell you. But I knew you needed to know. Thanks Abby. You always are the best person to talk too."

"Dinner!" My mom shouted, interrupting our conversation.

"Let's go?"

"Yep."

We both took a seat at the dinner table, joining my mom.

The whole time my mom and Abby kept talking and making jokes. I think they really hit it off.

After dinner Abby stayed for a couple hours and we all just watched a movie together. When the movie was over Abby had to leave.

"Well thank you so much Ms. Smith for the dinner, it was really wonderful, and thank you for having me."

"No problem sweetie. Anytime. You can come here even when Dillian's not here."

They both laughed.

"Well thanks Dillian."

My mom walked away.

"No problem Abby anytime. Thanks for listening."

"Thanks for trusting me."

She hugged me and kissed me on the cheek.

"Bye Dill."

"Bye Abby."

I shut and leaned against the door and slid down, leaving me sitting on the floor. She kissed me. That means she had to believe me, and she still liked me.

My mom walked back in after hearing the door shut.

"I liked her. A lot actually. Even more than you."

"Very funny. You love me. And I told you, she's different."

"She is, and I heard her response to what you told her. She seems like a keeper."

"She is a keeper. I just hope she likes me like I like her."

"She does, trust me."

"How do you know?"

"Because I know."

I shrugged my shoulders and smiled. I walked upstairs and texted Abby.

"Thanks for understanding."

"No problem Dill, anything for you."

I smiled and locked my phone. I put my phone down and fell asleep.

I woke up the next morning to a pounding sound on my front door.

When I got to the door it was Abby. With the police.

"Yep, that's him officer. He's the one who raped me *and* my cousin, Brittney."

ISBN   978-1-67819-847-3

Here's a look at Desiree Zizzo's other story.

Disappearance is a Different Type of Fear

When I was younger, I was happy. I was happy because I didn't have to fear. I didn't have to fear if my best friend was okay or if I'd be next. My best friends name was Marcy. Not that It's important to you, but it is to me. I want her name to go on, I want it to be known, I want it to live. I want people to care.

Marcy was my childhood best friend. We did everything together, whether it was going on trips together to eating dinner with our families together. We were supposed to go to Disney World but a week before we were supposed to leave, Marcy was reported missing. This event changed my life in ways I couldn't imagine. I didn't know why whoever kidnapped her chose her or if he wanted me as well and if I would be the next missing kid in the small town of Galena, Illinois. I didn't know if she was okay, or where she was, or if she would ever come back. Every single day I replay the day I found out she was missing in my head. I remember eating dinner with my parents at the kitchen table. Then hearing a knock at the door, and I thought it was Marcy, so I ran to the door, but it was her mother. Crying. Pleading. Asking if I knew where she was.

After about 2 years of Marcy's disappearance, she was found. Dead. Nobody knew who, how or why just yet. But this small town would soon get all of their answers, and it would change everybody. Forever.